This Little Tiger book belongs to:

_____

_____

_____

For Lyra, who has the brightest of smiles whatever the weather ~ A M

LITTLE TIGER PRESS LTD,
an imprint of the Little Tiger Group
1 Coda Studios, 189 Munster Road, London SW6 6AW
www.littletiger.co.uk

First published in Great Britain 2012
This edition published 2019
Text and illustrations copyright © Adria Meserve 2012
Adria Meserve has asserted her right to be identified as the author and illustrator
of this work under the Copyright, Designs and Patents Act, 1988
A CIP catalogue record for this book is available from the British Library
All rights reserved

ISBN 978-1-78881-520-8
LTP/2700/2736/0319
Printed in China
2 4 6 8 10 9 7 5 3 1

What a Mess!

Adria Meserve

LITTLE TIGER

LONDON

Pitter-patter!
Rain was tapping at the
windows and wind was
banging at the doors.
It was a **miserable** day.

"Our day out is **ruined**," Mouse sighed. "No mouse would put a paw out in **that** weather. I'd catch a cold."

"Don't worry, Mouse," said Bear. "We'll just have to bicycle **in the house!**"

Mouse went first. He pedalled around
plant pots and swerved between table legs.
   "Good idea, Bear!" he giggled.
"This is fun!"

Soon he was whizzing round.

"Wheee!"

"Me too!"

cried Bear, but Bear
was **very big** and . . .

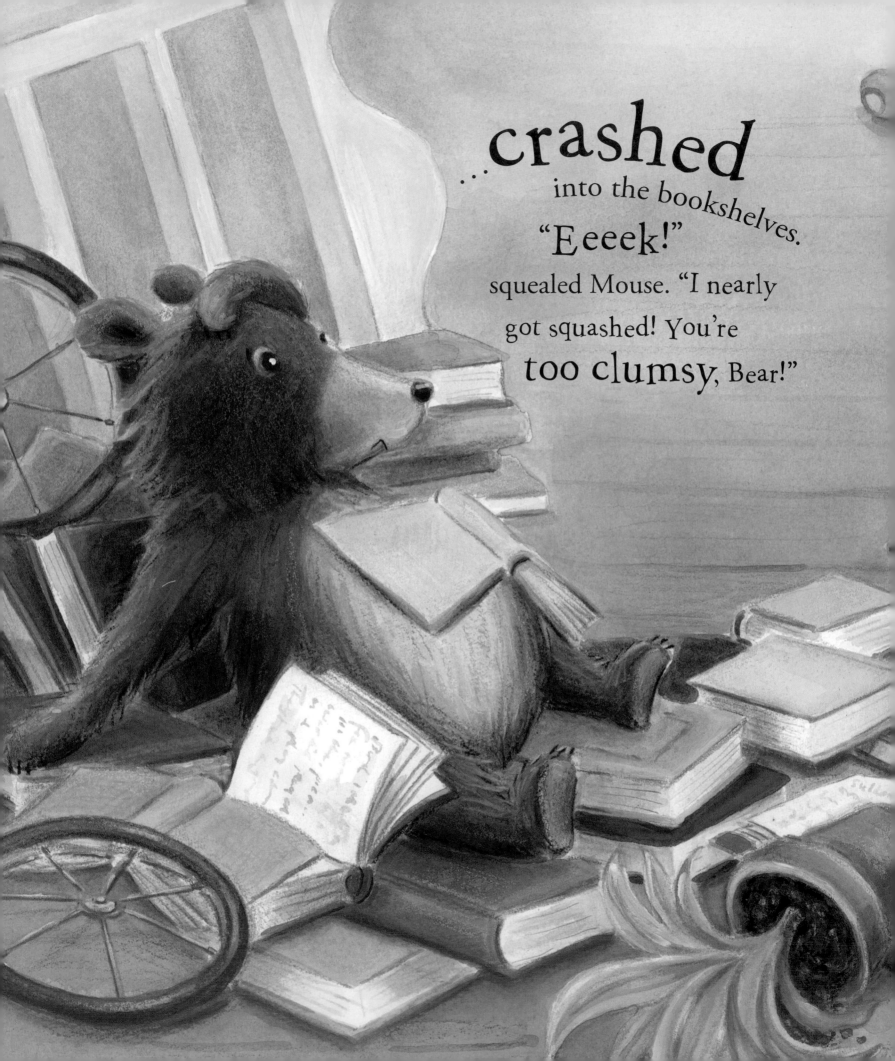

...crashed into the bookshelves. "Eeeek!" squealed Mouse. "I nearly got squashed! You're too clumsy, Bear!"

Poor Mouse. He **SO** wanted to play outside, but the rain was pelting down. Splish! Splosh!

"No mouse would put a whisker out in that," he sniffed. "I could get blown away."

"Don't be sad, Mouse," chirped Bear. "Let's build an indoor tree house!"

. . . knocked it all down.

Bang!

"You've **ruined** it," snapped Mouse. "You're just **too big**." "Sorry," sighed Bear, rubbing his nose. "But we can still have **our picnic!**"

"But we don't have cake," grumbled Mouse, "and we can't go to Rabbit's shop. No mouse would put an ear out there."

"No need to stamp your paws," said Bear. "Come on. We'll make our own cake."

Bear rushed around the kitchen gathering everything together.

Clink! Clank! Jangle!

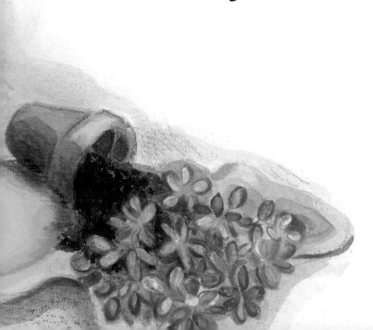

As they **measured** and **mixed**, Mouse forgot to be grumpy. And when they carefully poured the chocolatey, buttery batter into the tin, Mouse cheered right up.

But when the timer went ding!
and Bear took the cake
out of the oven
it went . . .

...flop!

"That's not a cake. That's a soggy mess!" shouted Mouse. "Nothing is going right today and it's all your fault!"

At that, Bear threw the cake out of the window! "Now it's a really soggy cake!" he roared. "And if I'm too big and clumsy then play on your own!"

Bear **stomped** off
and climbed back
into bed.

Mouse was squeakless.
He had never seen Bear so upset.
Without Bear bustling about,
all Mouse could hear was the
drumming of the rain and
the wailing of the wind.

"Bear?" Mouse called.
"Please come out and play..."
but there was no reply. There
was only **one thing** to do.

Mouse put a paw out in the rain.
It was cold. He put his head out.
The raindrops weighed down
his whiskers and the wind
whistled around
his ears.

But Mouse stepped out into the big dark wood anyway. "I could get snatched by a **monster**," he trembled.

Crack! He dodged a falling branch. Creak! Groan! Roar! A huge, scary shadow grabbed at him, but Mouse ran on.

When Bear got out of bed
he couldn't find Mouse
anywhere.

"Mouse said he would **never**
put a paw out in this weather,"
worried Bear as he tidied up.

"He could get **lost**," Bear
thought. "Or get snatched by a
scary monster!"

Bear **raced** out
into the storm, shouting,
"Mouse, come back!"
And then he saw…

That afternoon the rain still **poured**
and the wind still **howled**. But it
didn't matter. Bear and Mouse
had a **wonderful**
picnic inside.

As they ate their **delicious**
slices of cake, Bear and Mouse
clinked their mugs together:
"To best friends –
whatever the weather!"